MR DARCY

AND THE CHRISTMAS PUDDING

ALEX FIELD & PETER CARNAVAS

Written by Alex Field   Illustrated by Peter Carnavas

For Mum, with all my love. AF

For Peter and Sophia, with heartfelt
thanks for all you have done. PC

Christmas is the very best time of year, thought Mr Darcy.

Snow was falling as he hung the mistletoe
over his front door, making sure that there
were enough berries for everyone.

Perched on top of the ladder, Mr Darcy looked across Pemberley Park. Mr Collins was shivering behind the shed with his beady eyes firmly fixed on something.

Mr Darcy waddled over just in time to rescue his friend
Maria from the paws of Mr Collins.

Inside a roaring fire lit up Mr Darcy's great home.
It was a special day at Pemberley Park.

With Maria's help, Mr Darcy went to his kitchen to make sure he had
everything he needed - flour, currants, brown sugar and cinnamon.
Mr Collins was soon forgotten.

Caroline, Bingley, and Lizzy and her sisters all arrived for Stir-up Sunday.

They were busy finding bowls and spoons when they
heard a loud scratching at the window.

'What a noise!' cried Lizzy.
'It's Mr Collins,' said Mr Darcy importantly.
'He will soon stop.'

Lizzy ran to the window, followed by Bingley
and Caroline.
'Oh, he does look cold. Couldn't we invite
him in?' asked Lizzy.

'Certainly not,' said Mr Darcy as
Maria shook her head.

Mr Darcy went to the window to
close the curtains.

With the fire crackling in the background,
they all helped with the mixture for
Mr Darcy's famous Christmas pudding.

Each one of them took the wooden spoon
and stirred the mixture clockwise with
their eyes shut.

'Make sure you make a secret wish,' squeaked Maria as Lizzy
began to stir the mixture.

Lizzy looked out at Mr Collins.

Mr Darcy sighed.
'You can invite him inside, but only if he
promises not to scare poor Maria.'

Lizzy went outside to ask Mr Collins into the house
where it was warm.

Mr Collins was, as he promised, on his best behaviour. He never once snarled at Maria.

Mr Darcy and Lizzy handed out mugs of steaming hot chocolate for everyone, including Mr Collins.
They all played charades and soon forgot that Mr Collins had almost eaten Maria.

On Christmas Day, they all came back to share the pudding.

Afterwards, Bingley and Caroline took Mr Collins home where he could stay out of the cold and out of trouble. Lizzy's sisters soon followed.

The last berry on the mistletoe was left just for Lizzy.
She got her wish after all.